B10

Y0-EEF-307

DAY BY DAY WITH...

BEYONCÉ

BY
TAMMY GAGNE

Mitchell Lane
PUBLISHERS

P.O. Box 196
Hockessin, Delaware 19707
Visit us on the web: www.mitchelllane.com
Comments? email us:
mitche_____e.com

Mitchell Lane
PUBLISHERS

Printing   1   2   3   4   5   6   7   8   9

RANDY'S CORNER

DAY BY DAY WITH . . .

Beyoncé
LeBron James
Miley Cyrus
Taylor Swift

Library of Congress Cataloging-in-Publication Data
Gagne, Tammy.
  Day by day with Beyoncé / By Tammy Gagne.
    p. cm. — (Randy's corner)
  Includes bibliographical references and index.
  ISBN 978-1-58415-859-2 (library bound)
  1. Beyoncé, 1981– 2. Rhythm and blues musicians—United States—
Biography—Juvenile literature. 3. Singers—United States—Biography—Juvenile
literature. I. Title.
  ML3930.K66G34 2010
  782.42164092—dc22
  [B]
                                                              2010008957

ABOUT THE AUTHOR: Tammy Gagne is the author of numerous books for both adults and children, including *Day by Day with LeBron James* for Mitchell Lane Publishers. One of her favorite pastimes is visiting schools to speak to kids about the writing process. She lives in northern New England with her husband, son, dogs, and parrots.

PUBLISHER'S NOTE: The following story has been thoroughly researched, and to the best of our knowledge represents a true story. While every possible effort has been made to ensure accuracy, the publisher will not assume liability for damages caused by inaccuracies in the data and makes no warranty on the accuracy of the information contained herein. This story has not been authorized or endorsed by Beyoncé Knowles.

PLB

DAY BY DAY WITH

BEYONCÉ

Beyoncé is one of
the best-known
singers in the
world. She has
sold more than
55 million albums
as a solo artist,
and another
75 million as
a member of
the girl-group
Destiny's Child.
In addition
to singing,
Beyoncé is also
a very talented
songwriter, record
producer, dancer,
actress, and
fashion designer.

6

Beyoncé is a remarkable stage performer, putting on incredible dance shows. Her concerts include many different background dancers dressed in striking costumes. Beyoncé wears some outrageous outfits, too. The energy level at these events is contagious.

BEYONCÉ

Beyoncé also gets to be funny sometimes. In 2008, she appeared on *Saturday Night Live* with Justin Timberlake.

JUSTIN TIMBERLAKE

8

During a sketch on the comedy show, Justin and some other actors pretended to be female backup dancers in one of Beyoncé's videos.

Beyoncé signs an autograph for a fan in Sydney, Australia. She was visiting the country to promote her perfume, True Star. Beyoncé has fans all over the world, and she enjoys meeting as many of them as she can.

11

MOM

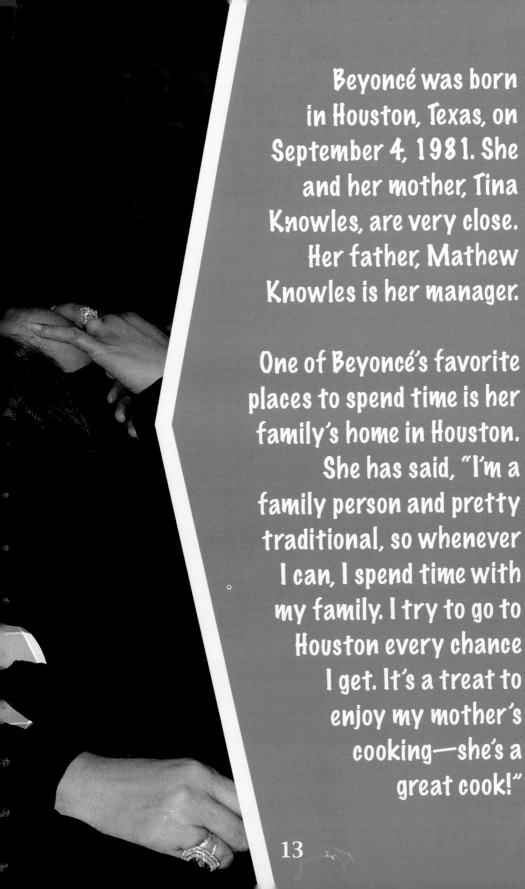

Beyoncé was born in Houston, Texas, on September 4, 1981. She and her mother, Tina Knowles, are very close. Her father, Mathew Knowles is her manager.

One of Beyoncé's favorite places to spend time is her family's home in Houston. She has said, "I'm a family person and pretty traditional, so whenever I can, I spend time with my family. I try to go to Houston every chance I get. It's a treat to enjoy my mother's cooking—she's a great cook!"

As mother and daughter, Tina and Beyoncé are also business partners. The two have a fashion line called House of Deréon.

BEYONCÉ WEARS UNIQUE SHOES

They showed it at Bloomingdale's in New York City in 2008. Beyoncé is also known for her love of shoes—especially high heels.

SOLANGE

Beyoncé is very close with her younger sister, Solange Knowles. Beyoncé and Solange grew up performing together, both on and off stage. When Solange was just a teenager, she became a backup dancer for Beyoncé's band Destiny's Child.

JAY-Z

Beyoncé's husband, Jay-Z, is a highly successful rapper and record producer. The two were married in April 2008.

When performing, Beyoncé pretends she is a character called Sasha Fierce.

She named her third solo album after this character. Her first two albums were *Dangerously in Love* and *B'Day*.

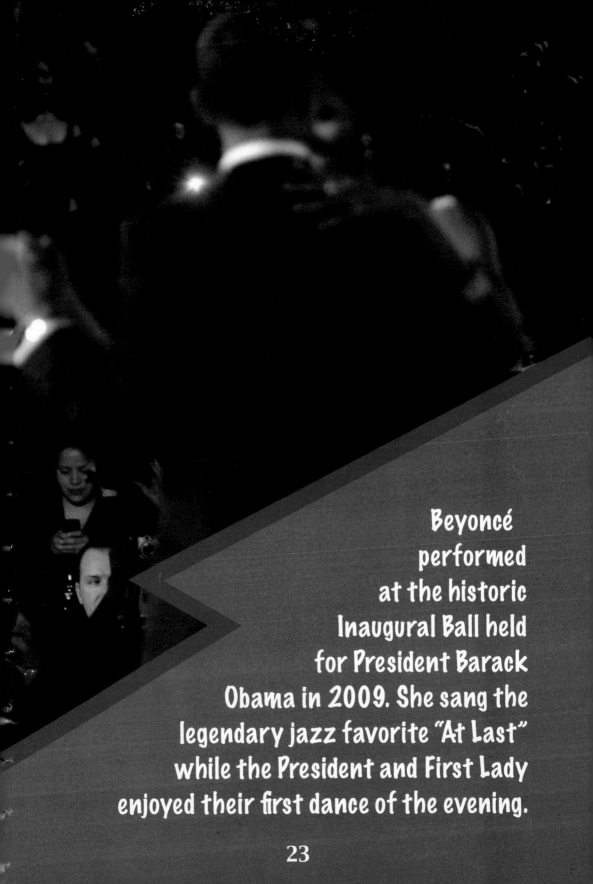

Beyoncé
performed
at the historic
Inaugural Ball held
for President Barack
Obama in 2009. She sang the
legendary jazz favorite "At Last"
while the President and First Lady
enjoyed their first dance of the evening.

Later in 2009, Beyoncé appeared at a memorial concert for pop icon Michael Jackson. Wearing an ultramodern white wedding gown–style dress, she sang a special version of "Ave Maria" and Sarah McLachlan's "Angel" at the event.

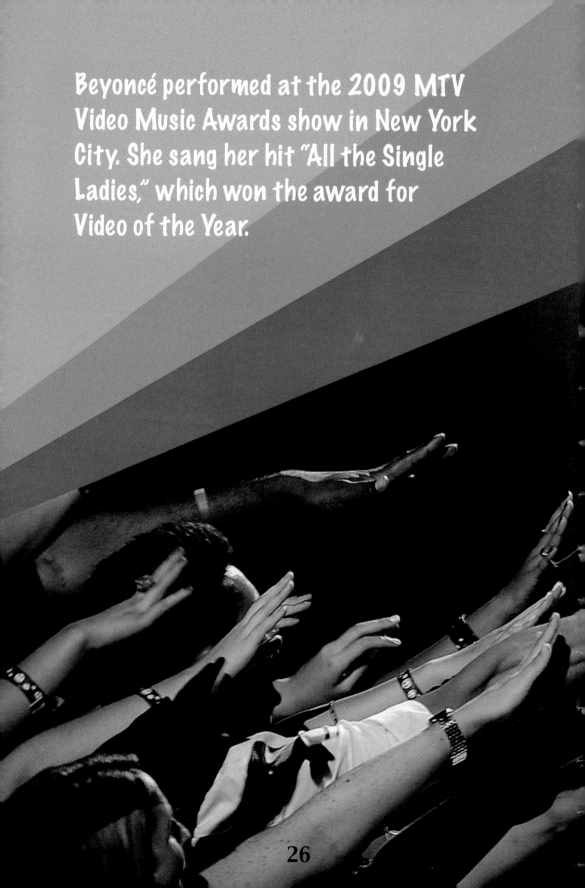

Beyoncé performed at the 2009 MTV Video Music Awards show in New York City. She sang her hit "All the Single Ladies," which won the award for Video of the Year.

Beyoncé uses her money and fame to help those less fortunate. She co-created Show Your Helping Hand, which delivers meals to food banks.

This campaign, which is joined with her Survivor Foundation, is working to relieve hunger in the United States. By early 2010, it had provided 2.8 million meals for people in need.

Beyoncé is a talented woman who is considered a triple threat in Hollywood. This means that she sings, she dances, and she acts. In addition to the many Grammy Awards she has won, in 2007 she was recognized for her acting role in the movie *Dreamgirls*.

Whether she is performing in front of presidents or helping to raise money to end hunger, Beyoncé is a true star.

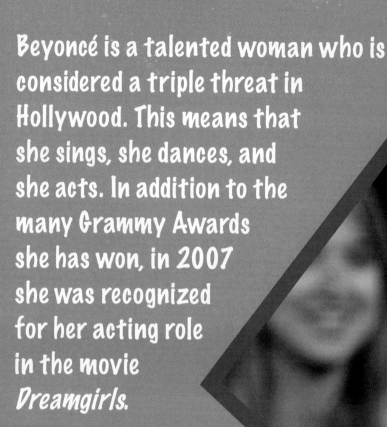

FURTHER READING

Works Consulted

Arenofsky, Janice. *Beyoncé: A Biography*. Santa Barbara, CA: Greenwood, 2009.

CNN. "Obamas Dance, Celebrate at Inaugural Balls." *CNN.com*, January 21, 2009. http://www.cnn.com/2009/POLITICS/01/20/inauguration.balls/index.html

Garcia, Jennifer, and Mike Fleeman. "Source: Beyoncé and Jay-Z Are Married." *People*, April 4, 2008. http://www.people.com/people/article/0,,20188764,00.html

MTV.com: *Beyoncé*. http://www.mtv.com/music/artist/knowles_beyonce/artist.jhtml

Books

Tieck, Sarah. *Beyoncé*. Edina, MA: Buddy Books, 2008.

Tracy, Kathleen. *Beyoncé*. Hockessin, DE: Mitchell Lane Publishers, 2005.

On the Internet

Beyoncé: I Am . . . Sasha Fierce
http://www.beyonceonline.com/
Destiny's Child Official Site
http://www.destinyschild.com/
Solange: Official Site
http://www.solangemusic.com/

INDEX